# Zombie Apo

## *How to Survive Apocalypse*

KIV Books

Copyright © 2017

Copyright © 2017 KIV Books

All rights reserved. This book or any portion thereof may not be reproduced or used in any manner whatsoever without the express written permission of the publisher except for the use of brief quotations in a book review.

## Disclaimer

This book is designed to provide condensed information. It is not intended to reprint all the information that is otherwise available, but instead to complement, amplify and supplement other texts. You are urged to read all the available material, learn as much as possible and tailor the information to your individual needs.

Every effort has been made to make this book as complete and as accurate as possible. However, there may be mistakes, both typographical and in content. Therefore, this text should be used only as a general guide and not as the ultimate source of information. The purpose of this book is to educate.

The author or the publisher shall have neither liability nor responsibility to any person or entity regarding any loss or damage caused, or alleged to have been caused, directly or indirectly, by the information contained in this book.

# Table of Contents

INTRODUCTION ............................................................................... 1

UNDERSTANDING THE APOCALYPSE ............................................ 2

YOUR ZOMBIE SURVIVAL KIT ........................................................ 8

SUSTENANCE ................................................................................ 17

WEAPONS ..................................................................................... 23

YOUR GAME PLAN ....................................................................... 31

MISCELLANEOUS SURVIVAL TIPS ................................................ 35

CONCLUSION ............................................................................... 40

# Introduction

It could be a viral outbreak. It could be a bio-chemical terrorist attack. It could also be a heaven-sent retaliation. It could even be a curse from a generation past, sent to make us pay for a long-overdue debt.

It's no longer a question if it's going to happen. It's more of a question of are you ready for it?

Unlike a nuclear apocalypse or collapse of a global market, the stakes are different when it comes to a zombie apocalypse. From preparation to everyday tactics, major changes should be made to ensure you outlast an outbreak.

This manual is designed to help you prepare and survive a zombie apocalypse. From telling you what to prepare to what to do, you'll know almost everything you need to make sure that you come out on top of such a catastrophe.

Besides provisions, materials and equipment, you will also read about survival mechanics during encounters to ensure that you walk away with your humanity in any given situation. In a world where everyone is trying to turn you into one of them, your sanity and humanity are your most prized possession. Here, you will learn techniques to safeguard those very possessions.

With proper preparation and training, you can become a stronghold for your family and loved ones when the time comes that humanity faces their last stand against their own former flesh.

# Understanding the Apocalypse

*"This is the way the world ends, not with a bang, but a whimper."*

*- T.S. Elliot*

The very definition of the word "apocalypse" is destruction on a catastrophic scale. What could be more catastrophic than the human race consuming itself in a zombie epidemic?

Many theories abound the web and modern media talk about how our untimely demise would be at our very own hands. The notion of a mind-altering condition that would turn humans into mindless eating machines has captures the imaginations of many people, hence the boom of apocalyptic TV series and video games.

## THE TRUTH

Putting aside pop culture and their symbolisms, a zombie apocalypse is no joke. It has several implications that will change the lives of survivors drastically.

Unlike a nuclear fallout and a global economic collapse, the threat won't come from the market or man-made machinery. It will come from humanity itself. A complete conversion from man to zombie will take place.

This means the stakes are different. For starters, you won't have to safeguard your physical belongings anymore. They will no longer be useful in a world filled with people whose only concern is to bite you.

Not only that, you don't just have a horde of zombies to worry about. There are also other survivors that might try to take advantage of you in order to steal your food and tools to increase their own chances of survival.

The whole dynamic changes once such an apocalypse takes place. When it starts, would you know what to do? How will you keep your loved ones safe as you try to get to safer areas?

## HOW WILLL IT START?

This is often the most difficult question to answer. Depending on the cause of a zombie apocalypse, it could happen gradually or it could also happen in a sudden outburst.

What could start as a simple case of bird flu could turn out to be the first mind-altering flesh-eating virus after a few weeks. Terrorists could launch a bio-chemical attack on a main city with a cultivated virus that turns humans into zombies.

This means your initial threat could come from anywhere. It could even start with you. If you're lucky enough to notice people acting out of the ordinary, don't be a hero and approach people right away. The close you are to a potential zombie, the closer you are to becoming one as well.

Just like with any apocalyptic-scale event, you will not have the chance to anticipate it. It will strike whenever it is supposed to whether you like it or not. This is why you need to have a direct plan of action when manure hits the fan.

## WHAT TO DO?

The very first thing you want to do is to get away from metropolitan areas. Remember, zombies used to be people. You do not want to be in an area with many people that could turn into a zombie encounter zone.

You may think it is better to stay indoors while you watch the rest of the world turn into zombies. That is the worst possible place to be. This is because you keep yourself in an area that will only get more and more dangerous over time.

You may be able to hide in your house for several weeks or even months. But as time goes by, the saturation of sane people in your residential area is only going to decrease unless your area gets military assistance and barricading.

That means the longer you stay in an urbanized area, the more zombies are going to be there to bite you. Your house will not stand a chance against a hundred mindless zombies banging on your doors and windows at the same time.

The only way you can stay safe in your own area is if you have a bunker or a panic room with in which you can hide. More details on these things will be discussed in a later chapter of this book.

Your primary condition is to lower your chances of encountering zombies and to get yourself somewhere safe. Cities, towns and villages are going to be out of the picture because you won't be able to tell if the people there are still people. As painful as it sounds, you will have to leave the comfort of your own home to increase your chances of survival.

The main goal is to get yourself as far away from crowded areas as possible. The lower the risk you're at of encountering the infested, the better chance you have of surviving.

Before that, you can set aside a change of clothes and an evacuation kit before anything takes place. Simply changing your clothes and grabbing this pack will multiply your survival chances tenfold. All it takes is some careful planning.

## WHAT TO WEAR?

Your main concern here is mobility and function rather than fashion. Throw out color schemes but don't disregard them as well. There will be a proper use of color coordination later on in this section.

For tops, go for something that is comfortable. Buttoned up shirts are no issue if you can run while buttoning them up. Shirts are better because they're easier to wear. Collared shirts really don't matter as long as you're alright with them.

As for fabrics, you will always want to go for clothes that let your skin breathe. Why? Because you'll never know when you'll need to start running. Sometimes, you will have to hide in the most inconvenient of places to avoid detection.

You'll never know where you're going to find yourself. The least you can do for yourself is to make your clothing as comfortable as possible. You'll be sweating a lot and get greasy and you might stay that way for prolonged periods of time without the chance to bathe.

As for bottoms, whether you're a male or female, you will always want to go for pants. Despite the need for mobility, you will also want to add function to your wardrobe as well. You might go for track pants or jogging pants, but they may not be as useful as other choices.

Go for pants with multiple pockets. You will be able to keep your knife, provisions, medicine, flashlight and other essentials immediately on you. You do not want to have to kneel and shuffle through your bag looking for a flashlight at night while a group of infected people are chasing you.

Another way to keep more items on you is to attach a small duffel bag on your belt area. That way, you can carry more essentials with you when you're out and about. If you have a gun, you will also need pants with loops that allow you to attach holsters and bullets.

As for shoes, you might be inclined to go for comfortable running shoes that will help keep you mobile. Although this is a good idea, you may also want to consider hiking boots or military footwear.

Take note that you will also be trying to avoid main roads and find yourself on the beaten path. You will be going through bushes and untouched areas where the ground could hurt your feet. A sturdy pair of boots will make trekking easier to reach safer ground.

On top of that, hiking shoes provide better stability in case of a zombie encounter. If you lose your balance while pushing zombies away, you're as good as one of them.

# COLORS

You may think that color schemes are of little importance, but that couldn't be farther from the truth. Remember the nature of a zombie apocalypse has no definite or defined grounds as of now.

With that being said, you won't know what nature of zombies there will be to avoid. With many different versions of zombies in different media such as TV, movies and video games, it's confusing to pick which archetype makes the most sense.

If the apocalypse started, would zombies be colorblind? Blind? Could they have heightened visual sensitivity? You really can't say. It could turn out in your favor or it could go horribly wrong for you. The best way to stay prepared is to anticipate for almost every possible outcome.

This is why it's advisable to avoid wearing bright colors that would attract attention. You may not be able to get clothes that also act as camouflage, but you want to be as inconspicuous as possible.

Go for neutral and earthy tones that mesh well with most outdoor backgrounds. This will help you buy as much time as possible to get away from almost any threat.

# HEADGEAR

It may not seem needed at the moment but you have to assume that you'll be on the road for long periods of time. This means you need something to protect your head from the elements.

You don't necessarily need a helmet, but you do need a hat. Go with something that is comfortable and provides adequate shade for your eyes in case the sun is up. You want to be able to travel fast despite the conditions. The longer you stay out in the open fields looking for shelter, the more you're at risk of a zombie encounter.

If you must bring shades, then do so only if you really need to. The thing with shades is that they distort your perception of the environment. They naturally dim the lights on your field of vision.

What if a zombie kid wearing black clothes was lurking in a particular corner? It would be hard to spot one right away.

You don't necessarily have to go Rambo and get everything in fatigue. What you're looking for is a nice harmony between comfort and function because of the nature of a zombie apocalypse. Comfort for when you're in compromising situations and function for difficult fixes.

Once you have that outfit selected, set it aside in your drawers or closet. You don't want to touch that outfit unless the zombie apocalypse has begun. After that, the next thing you want to take care of is your survival kit.

# Your Zombie Survival Kit

*"I am prepared for the worst, but I hope for the best."*

*- Benjamin Disraeli*

Now that your wardrobe is ready, it's time to prepare the rest of your person for the unthinkable.

## THE BACKPACK

This is the first thing that needs consideration. You want something comfortable and spacious at the same time. On the other hand, you don't want to have too much space as that will only weigh you down.

### Space

The first thing to look for in a backpack is space. Your survival kit is only as useful as the stuff inside. Weigh all your items and food and tools and see if you can find a bag that can accommodate the weight.

But you don't want a bag that can only handle as much as you want to bring. You will want some extra space in your bag. Pick one that has an expandable bottom or side to allow for more things along the way. You might pick up something important on the road like a map or a government document or more food items.

You will also want something with multiple compartments. It may sound confusing and fussy but it will actually help you categorize the items you place in your bag. Your food can go in one space, your tools can go in the other. Your maps and radios could go in another one as well.

### Comfort

Of course, you'll be lugging that backpack and its contents for long periods of time. You have to be able to do so with little discomfort. Fill the pack with clothing and try it on.

See if the straps dig into your shoulders. You're looking for a bag with very wide shoulder straps because they spread the weight of the bag across your upper half, making it easier to bring. You can also look for bags with waist support/straps and sternum support for added comfort.

If you have a large enough budget to spare, you can also invest in a military-grade backpack that can be expanded and carried around easily. It is also designed to be used under conditions such as rain and hail. They can also be worn while fighting and pushing away zombies.

## A Map

Be sure you don't just have a map for your city. Be sure you have a map of your whole country for that matter. You never know where the winds may take you. For all you know, everything to your right could be a zombie infested area.

As you cover more ground and discover more areas, you can mark them down on your map. You can also note your encounters and your observations. As time goes by, your map will become more and more valuable to the next person. You can end up bargaining with this treasure trove of information for food, water and ammunition.

## THE RADIO

Just because you're on the road and the cell sites and servers are down, that doesn't mean you can't get information on safe zones and other important updates.

Fortunately, radio waves are sturdier than internet routers. Despite radio stations going down, you can still pick up distress broadcasts or even messages from the government through certain frequencies.

The best kind of radio you want is a hand-crank radio. This may sound old-fashioned and burdensome but it's the most economical choice in an apocalyptic situation.

You may not have the luxury of passing by an abandoned electronics store or mall to scavenge for batteries. You don't even want to wander off into those areas unless you're sure they're zombie-free. A hand-crank radio doesn't need batteries and can be used whenever you need it as long as you can operate the crank.

## FIRST AID KIT

Fortunately, these come in packages when you buy them at any drugstore. They contain the most useful provisions for when you're out and about. Be sure to get something that comes in a sturdy case that is also weather-proof.

If in case you can't buy one, putting together the following items in one small bag will suffice:

A first-aid manual

Tape (adhesive for bandages)

Gauze Pads (different sizes)

Adhesive bandages

Splint

Soap

Antibacterial wipes

Alcohol wipes

Antiseptic solution

Toothache drops

Painkillers

Tweezers

Scissors

Safety Pins

Thermometer

The purpose of the kit is to enable you to administer first aid to yourself while you're out and about. You cannot always expect that you would have a doctor going around with you.

With the items above, you should be able to treat anything from wounds, bites, aches and pains that would make you less mobile in the dangerous outdoors. It would be anti-climactic if a simple toothache would be your undoing.

Since your kit will have some sharp items in it, a hard case should suffice so that they don't damage the rest of the contents.

You will also want to make sure that kit is one of the first things you can immediately see and grab from within your bag just in case of emergencies. An accessible kit can save lives.

## **RESPIRATOR**

This may sound like movie nonsense but you can't disregard the possibility of a zombie apocalypse being caused by an airborne biochemical attack. A respirator is your best way to stay healthy in such a case.

Another reason you will want a respirator is because you'll be dealing with humans that are potentially in a decomposing state. Worse, they could be turning into something else. There might be smells that could put you off and send you reeling to your doom if you don't have a respirator.

If you do not have access to one, a simple gas mask will be a good substitute. Chances are, you'll also find yourself in bad-smelling places where there aren't a lot of people. These will help you fight the smells.

## FLASHLIGHT

This goes without saying. You'll never know when you'll be sent out into the darkness from your campsite. You'll also want a flashlight just in case you get trapped inside a building without electricity.

You may not want to keep that directly inside your backpack, though. If your pack has some external pockets or slots, it should go there. It's even better if your backpack has pockets on the straps to make them accessible.

## MIRROR

You may question the logic behind this at first, but a mirror is indispensable in the right hands. You can use the mirror to blind attackers at the proper angles. You can also use the mirror as a signaling device for rescue helicopters should they hover near you.

## CROWBAR

Mostly used as a weapon in video games, a crowbar should be considered more as a tool. Because of its design, you can use it to pry open locked doors when you're trapped. You can also use it to open locked freezers or drawers to scavenge for supplies.

Of course, it's also good for hitting attackers in the head when you're trying to get away from zombies. Always strike using the business end of the crowbar to embed the sharp hook into their flesh to immediately dispose of them.

## TISSUE ROLLS

What will seem mundane and unimportant now will be indispensable during a zombie apocalypse. Tissue paper will be one of those things. You can't just wipe blood, entrails, grease and dirt off you with your hands. You're going to need something disposable to wipe yourself with.

You also don't want to be caught in the #2 position without anything to clean yourself with. You may be on the go but you still need to urinate and defecate.

## ROPE

You may need to fashion a make-shift weapon, rappel down a tall building or climb a steep rooftop. You'll need rope to do all those things. Keep several feet on your person just in case.

Besides those uses, you can also use rope to set-up traps, create detection systems and keep things together when you need to rest out in the open.

## BINOCULARS

These come in especially handy when you're in unknown territory. These things will help you scout the area to find any potential threats and ways to get through blockades from a distance.

## FLINT/WATERPROOF MATCHES

When night falls and you haven't found a stronghold, you still need to make camp and keep warm. Flint and a little tinder will help you start a good fire to keep your area dry and illuminated throughout the night.

Matches, on the other hand, are not as reliable as they can get wet and become useless. This is why you should go for the waterproof type so that they retain their utility no matter what the weather condition.

## IRON-CAST SKILLET

Although it may seem strange to bring cookware to the outdoors, this item serves a dual purpose. Naturally, you will be able to prepare better meals over a fire with a skillet. You may not need to eat your food items raw (which is always a better alternative). With a good fire, you can also take advantage of recently-salvaged perishable items such as meat and poultry, provided that they're still good for consumption.

On top of that, the skillet also serves as a good weapon. The large circular pan of the skillet makes it easy to use. A proper swing to the head of an attacker is enough to knock them off their feet if not dispose of them on the spot.

## SWISS ARMY KNIFE

They're small and come with multiple uses. From opening cans to cutting fingernails to picking your teeth, these knives are worth more than anything when you only have your wits about you. Be sure to keep one on you instead of in your backpack.

## COMPASS

If you find yourself in the wilderness as you get away from urban areas, you might become disoriented and lose your way. A compass will help keep you on track while covering more ground. The last thing you want is to get stuck in a strange area with no food or shelter.

## A DECK OF CARDS

Many online guides will advise that you bring one of these along. When you've found a stronghold or you've decided to go camping for the night, a deck of cards will serve as good distraction. Just because humanity is about to end, that doesn't mean you won't get bored while keeping yourself alive.

If you have the fortune of trusted company, a deck of cards becomes a good way to pass the time while waiting to be rescued. Even if you're alone, you can always play solitaire.

## A KNIFE

This last item should be one of the first things you should have. On top of being a reliable close-ranged weapon, knives are indispensable cutting tools for dead branches, ropes and even meat.

You don't necessarily need a fancy knife with serrated edges and everything. What you need is a cutting tool that you can keep on you both for utility and self-defense.

## TARP

While you won't be making any banners, these materials serve as great tents. When you decide to set up camp for the night, a few sticks and some rope with a tarp will keep you sheltered for the night.

## SLEEPING BAG

You never know how long you'll be travelling. Whether you've managed to secure a vehicle or not, you will need to sleep outdoors sooner or later. Just knowing you can bug out anywhere provides enough peace of mind to the wandering survivor.

Although it takes up a lot of space and adds weight to your kit, you cannot do without something soft to sleep on. Every opportunity to rest should be taken in order to replenish your energy for the journey after.

These preliminary items should create a good survival kit. These items alone should keep you mobile and alive for weeks to even months. Coupled with the right tactics and guides (which will be discussed in another chapter), you won't need to break into dangerous zombie-infested areas just to restock supplies.

Take note that your survival kit is not yet complete. Remember, you're a human being and not a drone. You need food and water to survive as well.

# Sustenance

*"Ask not what you can do for your country. Ask what's for lunch."*

*- Orson Wells*

Now that you already have tools and other necessities, it's time to worry about keeping yourself healthy and well-fed.

It's best to assume that most restaurants and grocery stores are full of zombies and expired food items. You do not want to endanger yourself just because it's lunchtime and you have no food. These suggestions will help complete your survival kit and help you avoid getting killed due to hunger.

## FOOD

This is the first thing you have to worry about. No matter where you are, your sustenance should always be the first consideration.

It also doesn't matter if you're in a stronghold or on the road. You will always only want non-perishable goods that can last for years.

At the core, you want to stock on food items that are easy to prepare, store and bring. Whether you're backpacking to a safe-zone or hauling up in a stronghold, you will need food items that need little maintenance and preparation. You'll never know when you need to get on the move in the middle of a meal.

## Astronaut Food

If you have access and the money to stock on these items, these should always be your first choice.

The best thing about astronaut food is that it's designed to keep astronauts healthy and full even in the harshest of environments: space. Imagine what good it would do for you on earth.

They have shelf lives for years and they're very easy to prepare. The only downside is the texture and their taste. These are menial inconveniences you should stomach for the sake of survival.

What makes these items better than canned goods is the fact that they're lighter. That makes them more backpack-friendly. They won't take up as much space for other necessities as well. These should always be your first choice.

## Tactical Sammich

Although not meant for astronauts, these items are intentionally designed for the worst conditions. From the name itself, these "sammiches" don't expire like the regular kind. Surprisingly, they can last up to two years in dry conditions.

They're also just as compact as astronaut food. They come in small sealed bags that can easily be opened with a knife. You don't even have to prepare them at all. Think of them as nutritional twinkies for soldiers.

The best part about them is that they come in different flavors. They pack about 300 calories a piece so that will keep you energized right after eating.

## Instant Noodles

These are the next best thing if the first two mentions in this list are out. There's also a larger chance you may like their taste better than the other two.

Just like astronaut food, instant ramen can stay in your shelf for more than two years. It will still taste the same as well as long as it isn't expired. This is because the food starts out dry, along with its flavoring and garnishes.

Despite those upsides, their preparation is a little more troublesome. You need to have hot water to prepare the noodles. The upside here is you get a meal and soup to go along with it. You just need a fire and a place in which to boil your water.

These things come in two varieties as well. You can get yourself packed noodles that come in a simple package that contains the noodles and flavoring packets. These are small and don't take up too much space in your bag.

On the other hand, there are also cup noodles that already come with a container in which to eat it. You just need the hot water and you're good to go. The downside here is that they're bulkier compared to their simpler counterparts.

## Energy Bars

They're light, which makes them perfect for your backpack. They're also ready-to-eat once you open them. They're no fuss and they give you energy on the go.

When you still can't set up camp but need to eat, these bars will suffice by instantly filling you and giving you a slight boost of energy to finally find camp.

## Assorted Nuts

A pack of trail mix can keep you fed for a whole day. These nuts fill you instantly as they're heavy on the stomach. They're also healthier than most other mentions on this list.

The only drawback to them is storage. If you open a pack, make sure you have a jar or a bag in which to keep them if you want to save them throughout the day.

## Biscuits/Crackers

You don't want to haul a large can of these around, but you want their handy packages. You can buy a pack of crackers in 3's that come packaged in plastic wraps. If you don't open them right away, they can stay good for months.

The only drawback to them is that they're fragile. If you keep them in a tight backpack you could end up crushing them within a few hours of walking. You might want to take a little precaution when bringing these.

## Canned Meat

One good thing about canned meat is its variety. There will always be a large assortment of these meats in any grocery store. You can choose from sausages, ham, corned beef, tuna and even sardines.

They also come cans which make them compact and easy to store. They're ideal for bunkers as well as lone survivors on the road. Sometimes, these cans also come with their own openers, making them even more convenient.

But the one thing you want about these items is that you don't have to prepare them anymore. You get the protein, filling and energy without having to start a fire.

Of course, they won't taste as good, but you're not out in the dangerous open for good food. You're out there to stay alive and find a safe place in which to live.

## Beef Jerky

Another ready-to-eat item, this one is easier on the backpack compared to canned meat. It's also just as healthy. It contains zinc and iron which are essential to stay focused during the end of humanity.

The only drawback to this item is its texture and sturdiness. You may have to chew a little harder but the taste is worth the trouble.

## Beans

Just as good as any other canned product, these items fill you just as much too. They have long shelf-life and are also ready-to-eat. They can serve as a complete meal in their own right.

You can also choose to cook them if you prefer your meals hot (and if you have the time). They're rich in fiber and other nutrients as well, making them a healthier choice.

## FLUIDS

It's not just about getting fed. It's also about getting watered and hydrated. You may already know this, but humans can go for weeks without food; but you'll be dead in three days without water.

## Bottled Water

This is the best kind you can get. It's processed, clean and ready for drinking. It's the availability that's the problem. You'll be sure that clean drinking water will become a premium item when surviving becomes the number one priority on earth.

Even if you can manage to scavenge a full grocery store, your supply is going to run out. A better way to procure water is to find a way to turn water from the environment into something potable.

## Water Filter Bottles

Thanks to the latest advances in filtration systems, many manufacturers have made it possible to perform portable filtration through water filter bottles.

Most of their mechanisms work the same way. You take dirty water (from streams, rivers, lakes and even tap water) and put it in the bottle. The bottles' filtration systems kick in with the help of gravity to purify the water, turning it into safe drinking water.

The only setback to these devices is that they take time to finish the job. They cannot instantly clean your water as fast as you want. Sometimes, you may have to wait a few minutes for a full glass of water. Despite that, they're worth the investment.

## Energy Drinks

Mostly overlooked as a cheap alternative to Gatorade, energy drinks are full of caffeine and sugar. These things may not sound healthy at first, but if you're about to run through an infested part of town to get out, you might want to have a sugar rush helping you out.

## Powdered Coffee

Even in pre-apocalyptic settings, people have already clung to coffee to get a jumpstart on their day.

Just using hot water, you can also enjoy a caffeine boost when you wake in the morning. It may not be as good as Starbucks, though, but it has the caffeine most coffee-people are looking for. It's one of the few things that can jumpstart your day, besides a sudden zombie attack.

Take note that all these food items are ideal for the survivor on the road. They're light-weight and can be carried over long distances. Despite that, hoarding large amounts of these items in a bunker or panic room isn't a bad idea either.

# Weapons

*"Weapons are like money; no one knows the meaning of enough."*

*- Martin Amis*

Sadly, any zombie apocalypse will not be complete without the need to defend yourself. No matter how good you are at hiding or surviving, you will have to eventually fight for your life.

You may find yourself fighting against a zombie or another human being who is threatening you. Whatever the case, it is best to have something to use to defend yourself.

You can forget about the martial arts at this point. Although it's true that you can train your body to become a weapon in itself, you don't want to give zombies the chance to grab any of your appendages.

## BLADES

These, so far, are the most realistic and effective means of fending for yourself. They serve as great extensions of the body and are designed to separate limbs from the rest of the body. The question is, what kind of blade are you looking for?

You probably already have a knife (or knives) at the ready. These can also be considered weapons but they're more useful than they are deadly. Fighting with a knife will force you to come into very close range with a zombie, where the chances of getting bitten are very high.

### Machete

What you want is something long that extends your reach, but not too long to become a burden when you're travelling. This is why most experts would advise a machete.

These are broad and heavy blades that aren't as long as most traditional swords but are larger than knives. On the field, they are well-known for being good at cutting down branches and other obstructions that are in the way.

This blade is easy to wield because it is shorter than a standard sword but long enough to allow you to swing from a short distance before a zombie can get a hold on you.

The best thing about a machete is that it does not have serrated edges like most knives. You may not know this, but serrated edges were designed to inflict pain and increase the size and intricacy of the wounds it inflict on people.

Sadly, you don't want to injure former people during a zombie apocalypse. You want to dispose of them right away. A serrated edge will increase the chances of getting your blade stuck in the flesh of the undead, forcing you to spend more time on a zombie that should have died with the first strike. That is time used for running away or killing the next zombie.

## Kukri

Hailing from a long history of Nepalese combat techniques, this unique blade is the second go-to melee weapon for a zombie apocalypse.

The main feature of this blade is that it has a forward curve, almost like a small scythe. The blade also widens at this forward curve, completing at least 2 feet for the smaller variants of this blade.

Because of the design, a swing with a kukri is heavier than a swing made with other blades. This is because the forward curve on the blade adds more weight to the direction of the swing.

This is the reason the blade is also used in farming scenarios. It can cut through branches and small logs easily. This also makes the blade ideal for separating appendages from a person. Cutting off a zombie arm is easier with a kukri compared to other larger blades that are heavier.

## Katana

This falls last on the list of desirable blades because of its availability. Not everyone may have access to such a blade or a blacksmith capable of making one, but their combat potential is quite scary.

Designed exclusively for the use of a trained samurai warrior, the sharpness of a katana is the stuff of legends. These swords have been known to cut through armor and flesh with the flick of the wrist, making them very deadly in the right hands.

This makes the blade an ideal weapon for immediately decapitating or slicing the head of a zombie, instantly felling them. These blades are much longer and require expert care, making them a high-maintenance weapon. Consider yourself very lucky if you get your hands on such a weapon for a zombie apocalypse.

## GUNS

Compared to a blade, a gun is more effective at disposing zombies. This is because you can kill one from afar as long as your aim is right. Also, the more powerful your gun is, the more zombies you can kill from a distance, keeping you safe while you clear a room or create an escape path for yourself.

Having said that, using guns entails two very distinct disadvantages. First, you run the risk of making noise when you use a gun. When you pull the trigger, you create a loud bang. That noise could attract wild animals or even more zombies to your position. Remember, you won't know if zombies are blind, deaf or even if they have heightened senses until the zombie apocalypse happens. As much as possible, you don't want to attract more zombies to you when you manage to put one down.

Another disadvantage you run with is the dependence on bullets. Take note, once the apocalypse starts, the number of available bullets on the planet suddenly becomes a finite number because there will be no one to manufacture them anymore.

This means you will eventually run out of bullets very quickly if you depend on them a lot. On top of that, you will have to allot space in your backpack for ammunition along with carrying the actual gun with you. That's added weight that could turn into a useless chunk of metal when you run out of bullets.

Despite that, there is no other way to effectively kill a zombie from a safe distance without the use of a gun. If you get your hands on one, it's best to bring it as long as you have a good supply of ammunition with you.

## Glock 17

Given the chance, you should ask for a Glock 17. This is because this is one of the easiest guns to use. You can train yourself on a 17 within 15 minutes. It's a pistol which makes it easy to bring and easy to aim, as long as you have steady arms.

On top of that, this gun is compatible with 9mm parabellum rounds. You will know this type to be the most abundant form of bullet in the world. You'll have larger chances of coming across these bullets more than any other kind during an apocalypse.

Police officers depend on this type of bullet for their pieces, which means you can stop by an abandoned police station for bullets with plenty of success; provided that you've cleared the area of police zombies.

## Shotgun

You will definitely want one of these in an apocalypse, especially if you've found yourself stuck in a high-encounter area. This is because shotguns can fire burst rounds. These shots spread in an arc from the tip of the weapon, hitting multiple targets over a wide area. That means one shot could floor a small group of zombies coming your way.

One of the best choices in shotgun would be any Remington model. These models are easy to use and they have long magazine tubes.

This means you won't have to reload that much after a series of shots.

## Hunting Rifle

If the shotgun is the preferred gun for hitting multiple zombies, the hunting rifle is the ideal weapon for shooting zombies from great distances.

With the hunter in mind, the hunting rifle has a very long range which extends up to five miles depending on the kind of rifle you have. That means you can shoot down a zombie from the other side of a football field and they'll never see it coming. Rifles also use more aerodynamic bullets, making their shots more accurate.

These guns are ideal in precarious situations wherein you have to shoot a zombie about to attack one of your loved ones. They're also used to eliminating zombie stragglers that are blocking your exit route.

You have to be careful not to go too far with your range and get a sniper rifle. These guns have the longest range but require you to stay in one position for a long time to get a good shot. You do not want to be caught on the ground when a zombie walks past by.

You may have also heard of machine guns and automatic rifles that shoot plenty of rounds in one go. You may have also seen these kinds of weapons take down large numbers of zombies in a matter of seconds. You don't want that.

First off, those weapons take up too much space and they're too heavy. They'll only slow you down. And when you slow down and encounter zombies, those guns will go through your entire supply of ammunition in a few seconds as well, leaving you with little choice.

Remember, you're not supposed to kill every zombie you see. In most cases, you won't have to if you plan carefully and choose your battles. Every escaped encounter is as good as a win in the game of survival.

Given that you're not that much of a gun expert, these three models will be the most user-friendly in case of a sudden apocalypse. You won't need to train for months on these guns in order to reap their tactical benefits.

One thing you have to remember, though, is that you only want to use guns when you have no other option. You do not want to waste bullets on killing zombies in a room you had no intention of entering. If you can escape or find another route, always go there. Less encounters means fewer bullets wasted and more time added to your survival record.

## OTHER WEAPONS

### Crossbow

This is one time you can believe in pop culture. Crossbows are ideal weapons for an apocalypse because they have recyclable bullets and they're quiet.

Just like Darryl Dixon, you too can kill zombies with a crossbow and pull the arrows back out when they're dead. You don't run out of arrows this way.

The only problem with a crossbow is that it's bigger than most guns. The bow itself already takes up plenty of space. You will also need a quiver for your arrows. If you can manage to get your hands on a tactical crossbow, you're in luck. But you have to put up with the added weight.

You can try leaving one of your other weapons behind. If you have a crossbow, chances are you'll be using that more than anything else because they're the most economical choice.

### Axe

This is a really good substitute for a machete or katana. They're heavy duty and they deliver a really good blow to the head with proper aim. If you're experienced with an ax, a sideways swing can also easily cut off a zombie's head.

On top if that, they're also useful for breaking down doors and wood walls. They can also be used to open small chests that have locks. With the right amount of force, they can give you access to new escape routes and supplies.

## Steel Bat

Never underestimate the power of blunt force. A good swing with a bat may not cut off a zombie head, but it's more than enough to knock them to the ground. On top of that, they're easier to wield.

With some creativity, you can also wrap barbed wire around the business end of a bat to add punctures along with blunt trauma.

You can also use bats to break through windows and doors like an ax.

## Nail Gun

This one makes it to list not because it's a powerful tool, but because there's a large chance that you already have one in your garage.

Although not as powerful as an actual gun with bullets, a nail gun can work wonders in semi-close range. Zombie heads are softer than wooden planks. Nails go through better that way.

It's even better if you have a battery-powered gun so that you can take it with you. There's a big chance you don't have any licensed firearms under your name as of yet. Nail guns are a good way around this issue if you haven't prepared yet.

# GETTING CREATIVE

You may not have a nail gun or even a steel bat at home, but that's alright. With the proper imagination and ingenuity, you can come up with your own customized self-defense tools.

Take a look at your surroundings and see what you can put together. A simple wooden plank with scissors attached to it can take out a zombie in one swing.

That lamp post that you have will be a good tool for pushing zombies away from you as you escape. You don't even have to remove the light bulb. You're lucky if you get to swing that at a zombie head.

The goal here is to find something with which to remove threats without using your arms and other appendages. You don't want to grab a zombie. You don't want to get close either. Anything long and sturdy will do, as long as they're not your arms.

# Your Game Plan

*"My zombie apocalypse plan is simple and effective; I plan to die with the first wave."*

*- Graham Parke*

Sure you're packed and ready to go. At this point, you probably have everything you need already. When the apocalypse starts, you know what to do. A very important question pops up at that instant.

## Where Are You Supposed To Go?

Forget about visiting relatives in other places or running back to province. Remember, you want to avoid urban areas to decrease your chances of encountering zombies.

It's not a question of where you should be. It's more of a question of how far away from zombies do you want to be. You want to put plenty of distance between you and anything that could potentially rob you of your humanity.

This could either mean in the wilderness or the countryside. Take note that you're not relocating yourself. You're preserving yourself by staying mobile and being hard to locate.

But you don't want to be wandering until you die of old age. At the very end, you want to be able to reestablish yourself in a community wherein you no longer have to worry about being attacked by a zombie. These communities are known as safe zones.

## What Are Safe Zones?

Fortunately, you're not the only one who wants to stay human. Very powerful people would also like to remain human and are more capable of creating a safe environment for people to live in despite more than half the world's population turning into mindless zombies.

Such people work in the government. Such people are high up in the government. They'll be the first people to try to create a habitable area wherein they can plan their defenses and create a usable form of communication to the outside world. These are what you call safe zones.

These are usually barricaded areas with armed guards at entrances. There are alarms and other detection devices that are operating to alert the people on duty if there are any approaching threats.

Inside, there lies the remaining forces of sane human beings who all just want to survive the apocalypse; people like you. Once you get out of your home and hit the road, your job is to find one of these areas and get in so that you can rebuild your life.

## Where Are They?

That will really depend on how things turn out during the beginning of the zombie apocalypse. You won't know who will make it or not when the world starts ending. That's why it's your job to remain mobile and alive long enough to be there when the dust settles and people start rebuilding.

This is where your hand-crank radio comes in. When a safe zone has established itself, one of the first things the people there will do is to see if there is anyone else who has created a safe zone or if there are any survivors out there.

When you set up camp, you don't want to be looking for good tunes on the radio. You want to browse through various frequencies to see if there is anyone broadcasting about their safe zones.

If your radio doesn't give you anything, you have to keep moving away from urban areas while keeping yourself alive. You have to earn yourself another day to use the radio to find your safe zone.

# OTHER SURVIVORS

There is also a high chance you will encounter other people with the same goals you have. This could be either a blessing or a curse.

On one hand, having another person in your company is a good thing. This is because you can pool your resources together and end up with more provisions and ammunition. You can also get more information because different people will come from different areas under different conditions.

On the other hand, you could end up on the short end of the stick and meet an unprepared and poorly-stocked survivor who will eat out a larger share of your provisions. You may not be able to learn anything from them as well.

Worse, you could be in danger. Take note, people change during stressful situations. What could be more stressful than the end of the world? These people could be out to rob you of your things and equipment, leaving you either dead or slow enough to get caught by zombies.

This brings in the question of whether or not to accept someone into your company. To answer that, you would really have to depend on your instincts here. If you ever so much have a slight inkling that someone could spell trouble for you, then you should trust your judgment.

# DELAYED GRIEVING

What if you do end up trusting someone and you two turn out to become really good friends? That would be a very ideal situation for you because you'll have good company in a person who cares about you.

You'll know someone has your back just as much as you have theirs. You'll be able to pull more ideas together and keep each other motivated and alert. This kind of company in an apocalypse is invaluable.

What happens if they die? What if they get bitten by accident? What if you took a wrong route and got ambushed and you're the only one who gets out alive?

The loss of a friend will feel the same way in any scenario. It is a painful experience; which is made twice as poignant when you're right there watching them die or turn into a zombie.

This is where delayed grieving comes in. Putting all emotions aside, you'll be experiencing a deficit by losing an ally; nothing more and nothing less. Because this other person is out of the picture, you are back to being alone again.

Unless you've been compromised as well, your first thought should be to keep going. There will be a very strong urge to give up at this point due to the loss of a trusted companion, but this loss is not enough to cause you to surrender to your emotions.

Soldiers go through these ordeals every time they step into the battlefield. They watch their friends die in front of them but they push themselves to move one, leaving the corpses of their dear comrades in their path.

Unfortunately, this is not something that you can learn from a book, but is one of the most important lessons you will have to learn. You probably won't just see your friends die at the beginning of an apocalypse. You'll also probably see a lot of family members fail to protect themselves and end up on the wrong side of humanity.

These events are enough to bring you to your knees in grief. You have to remember that you do not have time for that. You need to keep on going not because you're one of the few surviving members of your family, but because you're one of the last surviving members of your species. You will have plenty of time to grieve when you've found a safe zone.

# Miscellaneous Survival Tips

*"Humor can be one of your best survival tools."*

*- Allen Klein*

Now that you've read what you need to bring, where you need to go and what to do if you're not yet there, you will still need to learn a few more nuggets before you can consider yourself prepared for a zombie apocalypse.

## Cut Your Hair

It doesn't matter if you're a man or a woman. You do not want to have long hair in the event of a zombie apocalypse. For starters, long hair is harder to manage and is a big encumbrance in hot weather. They get greasy and stick to your skin and make you uncomfortable. You may not even find shampoo for a long time.

Another disadvantage of long hair is the possibility of it getting grabbed by a chasing zombie. And when you get grabbed by the hair, your head follows suit. You'll be one of them in no time.

It's not the time to be worried about looks. Your top priority is keeping yourself alive. Your hairs can grow back as much as you want it to when you've found safe haven.

## Pick Your Battles

What seems like expert parenting advice may also save your life one day. Remember, you're not there to exterminate zombies. You can leave that job to the military and the government. Your job is to stay alive.

Assess every situation and look at what you have. Will killing something be worth the trouble? Is there another way around a certain encounter? Do you really have to engage in this situation?

At the bottom line, the less encounters you have, the higher you chances are of still being human the next day. Do not waste precious energy and bullets trying to play a hero.

## The Sun Is Your Friend

You won't know if zombies can see in the dark until the apocalypse actually happens, and you certainly don't want to be the one to make that discovery. You only want to travel when there's light. You have one more sense organ working properly during the day. That alone improves your chances of survival.

Make it your daily goal to find a safe camping site by the end of the day. Ideally, that would be a place with several escape routes and deep bodies of water. You will also have to learn how to set alarms for yourself especially if you're travelling alone.

## Always Aim For The Head

When it comes to dealing with zombies, you can trust the anatomical build of humans to work to your advantage. Zombies may have lost their humanity, but their structure remains the same. All bodily functions still come from the nervous system whose control center is the brain.

This means you can immediately shut down a zombie by attacking the brain. You can either cut off its head if you have a good enough weapon or shoot it there if your aim is good enough. Do not try to immobilize them first and waste bullets and strength.

## Knock On Doors

This isn't just a polite policy. By knocking on a door before you enter, you can verify if the room is empty. You're lucky if no one responds. In the worst case scenario, you'll wake up a group of zombies to the door with your knocking. It's always better to be safe than sorry.

## Do Not Believe The Movies

Movie writers aren't zombie experts. In fact, there won't be any zombie experts until you're actually in a zombie apocalypse. Everything we know about zombies is fiction.

While there may be some possible outcomes that could happen in real life, never depend on what you see in pop culture. TV and movies are nothing compared to real life.

## Protect Your Feet

These are the only things standing between you and your application for zombiehood. Wear comfortable but durable footwear. You will never know what kind of terrain you'll be encountering once you start moving out.

During a zombie apocalypse, a blister or a sprain is the equivalent of death. If you can't run properly, you'll only slow other people down and cause your own demise.

Make sure that your first aid kit has guides on how to treat sprains, blisters and any form of feet injuries that could hamper your mobility.

## Learn How To Swim

This is not because zombies can't swim. You don't know that yet; but making yourself mobile over different terrain will always be an advantage. If you can cross a lake or a river on your own, you have twice as much chances of living than someone who needs raft or a boat with a horde of zombies chasing in the back

## Do Not Drive

You may be tempted to get into that Lambho with the keys in the ignition that's in the middle of the road. That's a bad idea.

Remember, cars run on gasoline and can only go on roads. Roads are signs of civilization; civilization that's been transformed into the undead. If you drive a car, you're only going to end up in another town or city where more zombies are waiting.

On top of that, cars are kill boxes for zombies. They're compact and leave you with no escape route should zombies be able to surround your vehicle. The person that left the Lambho on the road is smarter for leaving his ride behind.

The safest set of wheels you can use is a bicycle. They're quiet, they run on human energy and they can easily be abandoned when you need to go on foot. They can also help you easily outrun a horde that's only good at running towards you.

## Do Not Communicate Over The Radio

This may sound like bad advice at first, but it's a grim world out there, even without the zombie apocalypse.

You wouldn't trust a complete stranger on the road at first. Why would you trust a complete stranger over the radio? You may intercept broadcasts from other groups of people claiming that they're in a safe zone and that you should go there. You may have found your ticket to freedom or you could be walking into a trap set by bandits and thieves.

This is why you should only listen and protect your location. If you come across interesting news, try not to believe it first and let out the skeptic within you. Although welcome news is seldom doubted ocalyptic situations, take everything with a pinch of salt. You may be better off alone than joining a group that claims to be safe.

## Watch Your Numbers

If you're part of a group of trusted people and peers, you might want to monitor how many people you're travelling with. An ideal number for a group is about 4 people. Anything more than 10 people is a problem.

This is because large groups attract attention. Even if you all don't speak to each other on the road, your combined footsteps make a lot of noise. You will also leave more tracks. Sticking together may not be a good idea if you're that many.

You may also have to end up leaving your group if you feel you're too many already. This may sound like a difficult sacrifice, but you'll be better off without too many people attracting attention to your presence.

# Conclusion

*"What the Caterpillar calls the end of the world the master calls a butterfly."*

*- Richard Bach*

With the instructions in this manual, you are at your most prepared for a zombie apocalypse. Despite that, there are a few things you have to remember.

First, it's not going to feel like anything you've seen on TV or in the movies. Although zombie movies and shows do a great job of stirring our imaginations, they will never feel as authentic as the real thing.

You may feel excitement and clarity when you talk about zombies now, but when an apocalypse takes place, all that confidence will be replaced with fear and confusion, regardless of how many zombie outbreak movies you've seen.

Fortunately, the only way to combat fear is with knowledge. The tips in this book will help turn you into anyone's best chances for survival. While everyone is panicking and worried about what to do, you will remain calm and collected, keeping out of trouble and slowly working towards survival.

Try being an inspiration and help to other people by sharing this book with them and sharing your own thoughts on how to survive the apocalypse.

Printed in Great Britain
by Amazon